D0292033

Enjoy all of the Princess Posey books

PRINCESS P✿SEY

and the

FIRST GRADE BALLET

Stephanie Greene

ILLUSTRATED BY
Stephanie Roth Sisson

G. P. PUTNAM'S SONS
AN IMPRINT OF PENGUIN GROUP (USA)

G. P. PUTNAM'S SONS
Published by the Penguin Group
Penguin Group (USA) LLC
375 Hudson Street
New York, NY 10014

USA | Canada | UK | Ireland | Australia
New Zealand | India | South Africa | China
penguin.com
A Penguin Random House Company

Text copyright © 2014 by Stephanie Greene.
Illustrations copyright © 2014 by Stephanie Roth Sisson.
Penguin supports copyright. Copyright fuels creativity, encourages
diverse voices, promotes free speech, and creates a vibrant culture.
Thank you for buying an authorized edition of this book and for complying
with copyright laws by not reproducing, scanning, or distributing any part of it
in any form without permission. You are supporting writers and allowing Penguin
to continue to publish books for every reader.
Library of Congress Cataloging-in-Publication Data
Greene, Stephanie.
Princess Posey and the first grade ballet / Stephanie Greene;
illustrated by Stephanie Roth Sisson.
pages cm—(Princess Posey ; 9)
Summary: "Valentine's Day is coming! Posey is so excited about her special ballet
recital and giving cards to everyone at school. Then she learns that one of her
classmates doesn't have any valentines to give out. Can Princess Posey and
her tutu find the perfect way to help?"—Provided by publisher.
[1. Generosity—Fiction. 2. Friendship—Fiction. 3. Ballet—Fiction. 4. Schools—
Fiction. 5. Valentine's Day—Fiction.] I. Sisson, Stephanie Roth, illustrator. II. Title.
PZ7.G8434Pno 2014 [Fic]—dc23 2014004420

Printed in the United States of America.
ISBN 978-0-399-16962-5
1 3 5 7 9 10 8 6 4 2

Design and decorative graphics by Marikka Tamura.
Text set in Stempel Garamond.

For George

—S.G.

To Terry Joslin

—S.R.S.

CONTENTS

BALLET CLASS

"Let's try first position," Miss Julia said.

Posey stood up straight. She put her heels together and pointed her toes out. She curved her arms in front of her.

Ballet was hard. There was so much to remember.

Posey loved it more than anything.

She loved the studio with mirrors on the walls. She loved her pale pink ballet slippers. She loved skipping across the room to the music.

Dancing made Posey feel beautiful.

Gramps gave her lessons for Christmas. Next week, her class was giving its first recital.

A Valentine's Day ballet.

Posey's class was going to be hearts.

Miss Julia walked around the studio. "Elizabeth, heels together. That's right," she said. "Posey, remember to keep your head up."

Posey looked up. It was hard not to watch her feet.

When the class ended, Miss Julia told them to sit in a circle.

Posey sat next to a girl named

Caroline. Caroline was new at ballet, too. Posey didn't know the names of all the other girls yet.

Except Lin. They all knew Lin.

Lin had started ballet when she was three. She was the best dancer in the class. She wore her hair in a neat bun. Every week she wore a different colored net over it.

Posey felt shy around her.

"I know you're excited to see your costumes," Miss Julia said. She was holding a hanger behind her back. "Lin, would you stand up, please?"

Miss Julia slipped the costume over Lin's head.

"Ohhh . . . ," the other girls sighed.

There was a large red heart on Lin's front. There was one on her back, too. Sparkly ribbons dangled from the top and sides.

"You tie the ribbons here and here." Miss Julia tied bows on Lin's shoulders and at her waist. "Everyone will also wear one of these."

She held up a skirt. It was made of red netting.

Posey thought it was the most beautiful costume in the whole world.

"You can try on your costumes

at rehearsal on Saturday," Miss Julia said. "It will be our last rehearsal before the recital."

The girls went into the coatroom to change into their boots.

"My mom's going to buy me a new leotard," Lin said.

"So is my mom," said Angel.

"Mine, too," said a girl with a dark braid.

Posey would ask her mom, too. She could hardly wait to dance in her beautiful Valentine's Day costume.

"I WOULDN'T MISS IT FOR THE WORLD"

"The hearts are made of velvet," Posey explained when Gramps picked her up. "They're very soft. And there's a red skirt."

"Sounds pretty fancy," said Gramps.

"It's going to be so beautiful." Posey sighed happily.

"You'll be the prettiest heart there," said Gramps.

"MOO!" Danny kicked his feet against his car seat and said it again. "MOO!"

Danny loved to make animal noises. He thought he was so funny.

"Do an owl," Posey told him.

"WHOO, WHOO!" said Danny.

Posey and Gramps laughed.

When they got home, Posey asked, "Do you think Mrs. Romero will come to my recital?"

"You won't know until you invite her," said Gramps.

"I'll go right now!"

Posey ran next door to Mrs. Romero's house. Gramps had shoveled a path through the snow.

Posey knocked on the kitchen door.

"Come in!" Mrs. Romero called.

Posey took off her boots and put them on the small rug inside the door. She went into the living room.

"It's me," she said.

"Hi, you." Mrs. Romero was drying her dog, Hero, with a towel. He wiggled and squirmed.

"Hero got wet playing in the snow," Mrs. Romero said. "He's such a little baby when I have to dry him off."

"A big baby, you mean." Posey put her arms around Hero's neck.

"How was ballet?" Mrs. Romero asked.

Posey told her about the recital. And her costume.

"Everyone's going to wear a new leotard," Posey said. "Will you come and watch?"

"I wouldn't miss it for the world," said Mrs. Romero.

POSEY'S DISAPPOINTMENT

Posey's mom had to work until seven o'clock. Gramps ate dinner with Posey and Danny.

When they finished, Posey went upstairs to put on her pajamas. She lined up her stuffed animals on her bed.

She showed them the first position. She pointed her toes.

"We have to talk French, too," Posey told them. "*Demi plee-ay* means 'bend your knees.' You're not supposed to look at your feet."

The animals clapped and cheered.

Posey heard Danny yell. Then she heard her mom's voice.

She ran down the stairs and into the kitchen.

"You won't believe it, Mom!" Posey cried. "It's the most beautiful costume you ever saw! And you know what?"

"Hold on, Posey. Give me a minute to take off my coat," her mom said.

Gramps had left. He beeped his horn as he drove past the kitchen window.

Danny was clinging to their

mom's legs. It was his bedtime, so he was cranky. Posey's mom filled his sippy cup with water and gave it to him.

"Now, what did you want to tell me?" she asked Posey.

Posey told her about the heart costume and the new leotard.

"There's nothing wrong with the leotard you have," said her mom.

"Everyone else is getting a new one," Posey said.

"I'm sorry, Posey. I don't have the money to buy a new leotard right now," her mom said.

"I need one!" Posey cried.

"Posey . . ."

Posey blinked hard. She wiped her eyes with her hands.

"You don't need one, you want one," her mom said calmly. "That's different."

"But Mom . . . !"

Danny threw his cup on the floor and held up his arms. "Uppy, uppy," he cried.

Posey's mom picked him up.

"It's late and we're all tired," she told Posey. "Let's go brush your teeth. After I put Danny to bed, we'll read a book."

"How come Danny always gets what he wants?" Posey sniffed.

"Because all he wants is a hug." Her mom smiled and held out her arm. "Would you like a hug, too?"

"No."

Posey didn't want a hug. She wanted a new leotard so she would be like everyone else.

CHAPTER FOUR

VALENTINE'S DAY MAILBOXES

The next day at school, they made mailboxes with faces to hold their valentines.

Everyone brought in a cardboard box. They covered the boxes

with colored paper. They cut holes in one side for the mouth. That's where the cards would go.

Miss Lee said they could make their face be anything they wanted.

They cut teeth out of paper and glued them on. They glued on eyebrows and eyes.

Posey and Ava and Nikki and Grace worked together on theirs.

"Mine's a fancy lady, so I'm putting on lipstick," Posey said. She drew lips around the mouth with red crayon.

"Mine is, too," said Ava. "Her lipstick's blue."

"If she had nails, she'd wear blue nail polish," Grace said.

"I'm giving mine curly hair," said Nikki.

Luca and some of the boys made monster mailboxes. They gave them sharp black teeth and feather beards.

"Me want more cards," Luca growled.

"Me eat all your cards," said Nate.

They banged their boxes together and pretended their monsters were fighting.

"Luca and Nate, be careful with those," said Miss Lee.

"I'm putting my favorite cards on my bulletin board in my room," Posey said.

"I'm saving my mailbox to put things in," said Ava.

"Remember to write your name on your mailbox in big letters," Miss Lee called.

Posey drew little hearts on hers. She pretended they were tattoos.

"I'm giving the funniest valentines," said Ava. "They're

lollipops that have capes like Wonder Woman."

"My brother's giving lollipops, too," Grace said. "Except his are Superman."

"Time to clean up," Miss Lee called. "Make sure you wash your hands before you get in line for lunch."

"Me hungry for hot dogs!" growled Luca's monster.

THE MEANING
OF POOR

After lunch, Miss Lee's class went to the playground. Everyone still wanted to talk about Valentine's Day.

"I save the cards I get from the girls, but not the boys," said Grace.

"I wrote 'love' on my cards to the girls," Ava said.

"If you write 'love' to the boys, they will think you *looooove* them," Posey said.

"They'll want to kiss you." Grace giggled.

"Yuck!" Nikki cried. "Mushy, mushy!"

"My hand feels broken from writing so many cards," said Grace.

Miss Lee had sent home a class list. It had twenty-four names. They had to give a card to everyone.

"What about Jade?" Ava said. "She doesn't even know anyone. How can she give cards?"

They looked over at a girl sitting on a bench by herself. She had long yellow hair. It hung in her face.

Jade had only been in Miss Lee's class for a few weeks. She didn't talk to anyone.

She didn't look at anyone or raise her hand.

"All she does is look at the ground," said Grace.

"I don't even know what her eyes look like," Posey said.

"Me, either," said Ava.

"Jade's not giving any cards," Nikki said.

"Why not?" asked Grace.

"She's poor." Nikki said it in a hushed voice like it was serious.

"What does that mean?" asked Ava.

"She said her mom doesn't have any money." Nikki's eyes were huge.

"I would be so sad if my mom didn't have money," said Grace.

"Me, too," said Ava.

Posey didn't say a word. A scared feeling had filled her body from her head to her toes.

It made her feel cold.

Her mom didn't have money to buy a leotard.

Did that mean Posey was poor, too?

COUNTING RICHES

Posey didn't ask her mom all afternoon. She was afraid of what her mom might say.

When it was bedtime, she tried to fall asleep. Her eyes kept popping open.

After a long time, her mom turned off the lights downstairs. She tiptoed into Posey's room to kiss her good night.

"What are you doing still awake?" said her mom.

"Can I ask you something?" Posey said.

"Of course." Her mom sat on the bed.

"Are we poor?"

"Good heavens, no." Her mom sounded surprised. "Why would you think that?"

"Because of my leotard." Posey's mouth felt trembly.

"Oh, Posey," her mom said quietly. "Not being able to buy whatever you want, the minute you want it, is very different than being poor. We're not poor—we're rich!"

"We are?"

"Just think of all the riches we have."

"Like what?"

"Well, for starters, we have you, and me, and Danny," her mom said. "And Gramps."

"And Mrs. Romero and Hero," said Posey.

"That's right. And our cozy little house and our nice backyard."

"And the tree house Gramps

is going to build for Danny and me."

"And food in our refrigerator and heat when we need it," her mom said.

"I like using the fireplace." Posey yawned. "It smells good."

"I don't want you to ever feel sorry for yourself when you can't have something you want," her mom said. "There are too many truly poor children in the world."

Like Jade, Posey thought.

"Feel better now?" her mom asked.

Posey nodded.

Her mom tucked Posey's blankets tight around her. "If you use all of your fingers and all of your toes, I bet you will still have more riches to count. Now go to sleep."

Her mom left the door open a

crack. Posey burrowed under her covers.

She held up one finger. My warm bed, she counted.

And Ava and Nikki and Grace . . . that was three more fingers. And Miss Lee.

And all of her animals. Poinky and Hoppy and Kiki and Roger.

And her doll, Wah.

Posey was out of fingers. She rolled onto her side and closed her eyes. She tried to count on her toes.

She had her tutu that made her feel brave. She wiggled her big toe.

And reading books. And school. That was two more toes.

And drawing . . .

And dancing . . .

And the birds that came to their bird feeder . . . and the sun that made the flowers grow . . .

And . . .

And . . .

And . . .

Posey was asleep.

CHAPTER SEVEN

THE MEANING
OF HEARTS

At their rehearsal on Saturday, they were all excited to try on their costumes.

"Posey, this looks right for you," said Miss Julia.

Posey slipped the hearts over her head. Miss Julia's assistant tied the bows.

Posey stepped into her red skirt and looked at herself in the mirror. She turned around so she could see the heart on her back.

She felt beautiful.

Miss Julia put on the music.

"Remember that you're hearts!" she called. "Hearts mean love and kindness! Generosity! Put those feelings into your dance!"

Posey *did* feel those feelings. Everywhere she looked, girls in red hearts were dancing in the mirrors. They twirled. They leaped. They lifted up their arms and bent their knees.

They were real ballerinas.

Mrs. Romero was waiting for Posey in the coatroom after class.

"Why are you here?" Posey asked.

"Your mom and Gramps took Danny shopping," Mrs. Romero said. "I said I would pick you up."

Posey told Mrs. Romero about the rehearsal on the way home.

"Being a heart is very important," Posey said.

"It certainly is," said Mrs. Romero. "Love and kindness are what Valentine's Day is all about."

"That reminds me!" said Posey.
"Are you giving Gramps a Valentine's card?"

"I am." Mrs. Romero smiled.
"Can you keep a secret?"

Posey nodded.

"I'm giving him a windmill for his garden, too."

"Gramps loves windmills," said Posey. "Does that mean you love him?"

Mrs. Romero laughed. "I love *all* of you," she said.

"That means you do," Posey sang.

AS BRAVE AS
SHE COULD BE

"**H**ow are you doing on your valentines?" Posey's mom asked the next day.

"This is my last envelope." Posey wrote the name and put her pencil on the kitchen table.

"You still have to sign all of the cards," said her mom.

"I know that."

Danny was watching an animal show in the living room. Every time an animal made a sound, Danny did, too.

"ROAR!" he shouted.

"He thinks he's a real lion," said Posey.

"He acts like a real lion some of the time," her mom said.

"Mom, what does *generosity* mean?" Posey asked.

"Where did that come from?"

Posey told her about Miss Julia.

"Generosity means being kind," her mom said. "Giving to people who may not have as much as you do."

"That's what I thought." Posey put her envelopes in a pile. "There's a girl in my class who doesn't have valentines."

"Oh, dear. I'm so sorry," said her mom. "Does Miss Lee know?"

"I'm not sure."

"If you tell her tomorrow, she'll do something about it," her mom said.

Posey went up to her room.

She didn't want Miss Lee to do something about it. She wanted to do something about it by herself.

Posey put on her pink tutu and her veil and stood in front of her mirror. She looked at herself for a long time.

She knew what Princess Posey would do.

She would give her cards to Jade because of generosity.

That would be so hard.

Posey was afraid it would make her cry.

She wanted to be as brave as Princess Posey, but she wasn't sure that she could.

"DO YOU WANT
TO SHARE?"

The next day, Posey went to Jade's table just before lunch. Jade was drawing a picture.

"Do you want to see something, Jade?" she asked.

Jade didn't look up.

Posey took her cards out of her pack. "These are my valentines. I can't give them to you because then I won't have any," she said. "So do you want to share them?"

Jade kept drawing. Her long hair hid her face like a curtain.

Posey leaned down until her

cheek almost touched the table. She tried to see Jade's face.

"We can put both our names," Posey said. "Do you want to?"

The curtain shook back and forth.

"Posey and Jade, do you need some help?"

Posey sat up.

It was Miss Lee.

"Jade doesn't have valentines, so I asked her if she wants to share mine, but she said no," Posey told her.

"Oh, I see," said Miss Lee. "That was very kind of you, Posey. Do you think maybe Jade would like her own cards?"

"I'll check."

Posey put her head against the table again. "Jade, do you want your own cards?"

Jade finally looked at her. Her eyes were blue.

Posey sat up. "She does."

"Okay, then." Miss Lee held out her hand. "Jade, if you come with me, I have cards I can print out and you can color. Would you like that?"

Jade nodded. She stood up and took Miss Lee's hand.

"Posey, why don't you and Jade stay here during lunch and finish up your cards?" Miss Lee said.

"Okay."

Posey went and got her lunch bag. Jade came back with her

lunch tray. Miss Lee put scissors and a box of markers and crayons on the table between them.

Then she left them alone.

Posey unpacked her sandwich. "You know what I did one time?" she said.

She told Jade about Hero. About the time she had to push Hero's paw back through the fence. How scared she was that Hero might bite her.

Jade didn't say anything. But Posey could tell she was listening.

THE VALENTINE'S
DAY BALLET

On Valentine's Day, Gramps and Mrs. Romero drove Posey to her recital after school. She held her mailbox in her lap in the backseat. She lifted it up and shook it.

"I have twenty-four cards in here," Posey said.

"You'll have to wait to open those when you get home," said Gramps.

They parked at the ballet school. Posey looked at all the cars. Butterflies fluttered their wings in her stomach.

"Mom and Danny aren't here," she said.

"Don't you worry. Your mom was getting out of work early," said Gramps.

"What if she's late?" Posey asked.

"She'll be here," said Mrs. Romero.

They went inside.

"Go on, now," Gramps said. He gave Posey a gentle nudge. "Go put on that beautiful costume."

Posey hurried to the studio. All the girls were getting dressed. The air felt like electricity.

Miss Julia gave Posey the costume with her name pinned on it. The assistant tied Posey's bows.

Caroline was already dressed. "Something's wrong with Lin," she said.

Lin was sitting on a chair. She looked as if she was going to cry.

Posey went over to her. "Do you  have a scared stomach?" she asked.

Lin shook her head. "My net got a hole in it. I can't wear it." She held it up.

"That's okay. I'm wearing my

old leotard," Posey said. "We'll still be beautiful."

"We will?"

"Of course. Because dancing makes us so happy," Posey said.

Then it was time for them to line up.

No one talked. They filed down the hall to the stage. It sounded like there were a hundred million people in the auditorium.

Posey wished she could see her mom. What if she didn't get here? What if she missed Posey's first ever recital?

Miss Julia stopped at the curtain. The line stopped behind her.

"Big breaths, everyone," Miss Julia whispered. She took a deep breath and held it to show them. The little girls did, too. They all let their breaths out at the same time.

Miss Julia turned and walked out into the lights.

The audience hushed. It was so quiet.

Someone coughed.

Then Posey heard a sound that
made her eyes open wide.

"MOOOOO!"

They made it! All of her riches were here.

Posey followed the ballerinas onto the stage and danced with all of her heart.

Watch for the next **PRINCESS POSEY** book!

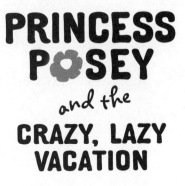

PRINCESS POSEY
and the
CRAZY, LAZY VACATION

When Posey's mom says they are going to have a lazy spring vacation at home, Posey is worried she won't have any fun. But her first loose tooth, a new bike, a sleepover at Nikki's, and an adventure with Gramps prove her wrong. Turns out it's impossible for a first grader to have a boring vacation!